187224

PowerKids Readers:

The Bilingual Library of the United States of America™

Bilingual Edition
English/Spanish
Edición bilingüe

KENTUCKY

VANESSA BROWN

TRADUCCIÓN AL ESPAÑOL: MARÍA CRISTINA BRÚSCA

The Rosen Publishing Group's
PowerKids Press™ & **Editorial Buenas Letras**™
New York

Published in 2006 by The Rosen Publishing Group, Inc.
29 East 21st Street, New York, NY 10010

First Edition

Layout Design: Thomas Somers

Photo Credits: Cover © Bob Krist/Corbis; p.5 © Kevin R.Morris/Corbis; pp.5,30 (State seal) © One Mile Up, Inc.; p.7 © Geo Atlas; pp.9,30 (Bluegrass state), 31(meadow) © Ric Ergenbright/Corbis; p.11 © David Muench/Corbis; p.13 © Kevin Fleming/Corbis; pp.15,31 (Boone) © Corbis; pp.17,31 (Lincoln) © Bettmann/Corbis; p.19 © Tim Mosenfelder/Corbis; p.21 © Raymond Gehman/Corbis; p.23 © Rick Rickman/NewSport/Corbis; pp.25, 30 (Frankfort) © Kevin R. Morris/Corbis; pp.26, 30 (Poplar) © Lee Snider/Photo Images/Corbis; pp.30 (Goldenrod), 31(stem) © Wolfgang Kaehler/Corbis; p.30 (Cardinal) © Gary W. Carter/Corbis; p.31(Brown) © Hulton Archive/Getty Images; p.31(Lynn) © Ron Sachs/Corbis; p.31(Ali) © Lynn Goldsmith/Corbis; p.31(Meagher) © Tony Duffy/Staff/Getty Images; p.31(slavery) © Hulton-Deutsch Collection/Corbis.

Library of Congress Cataloging-in-Publication Data

Brown, Vanessa, 1963–
Kentucky / Vanessa Brown ; traducción al español, María Cristina Brusca.— 1st ed.
p. cm. — The bilingual library of the United States of America) Includes bibliographical references (p.) and index.
ISBN 1-4042-3082-3 (library binding)
1. Kentucky—Juvenile literature. I. Title. II. Series.
F451.3.B765 2006
976.9—dc22

2005006102

Manufactured in the United States of America

Due to the changing nature of Internet links, Editorial Buenas Letras has developed an online list of Web sites related to the subject of this book. This site is updated regularly. Please use this link to access the list:

http://www.buenasletraslinks.com/ls/kentucky

Contents

1 Welcome to Kentucky 4
2 Kentucky Geography 6
3 Kentucky History 12
4 Living in Kentucky 18
5 Let's Draw Kentucky's State Tree 26
Timeline/Kentucky Events 28–29
Kentucky Facts 30
Famous Kentuckians/Words To Know 31
Resources/Word Count/Index 32

Contenido

1 Bienvenidos a Kentucky 4
2 Geografía de Kentucky 6
3 Historia de Kentucky 12
4 La vida en Kentucky 18
5 Dibujemos el árbol del estado de Kentucky 26
Cronología/Eventos en Kentucky 28–29
Datos sobre Kentucky 30
Kentuckianos Famosos/Palabras que debes saber 31
Recursos/Número de palabras/Índice 32

Welcome to Kentucky

These are the flag and the seal of Kentucky. The navy blue flag has the state seal in the center. The seal has the state motto. It says "United We Stand, Divided We Fall."

Bienvenidos a Kentucky

Estos son la bandera y el escudo de Kentucky. La bandera, de color azul marino, tiene en el centro el escudo del estado. En el escudo está el lema del estado. El lema nos recuerda que la unión hace la fuerza.

Kentucky Flag and State Seal

Bandera y escudo de Kentucky

Kentucky Geography

Kentucky borders the states of Missouri, Illinois, Indiana, Ohio, West Virginia, Virginia, and Tennessee. Kentucky's northern border is formed by the Ohio River.

Geografía de Kentucky

Kentucky está limitado por los estados de Misuri, Illinois, Indiana, Ohio, Virginia Occidental, Virginia y Tennessee. La frontera norte de Kentucky está formada por el río Ohio.

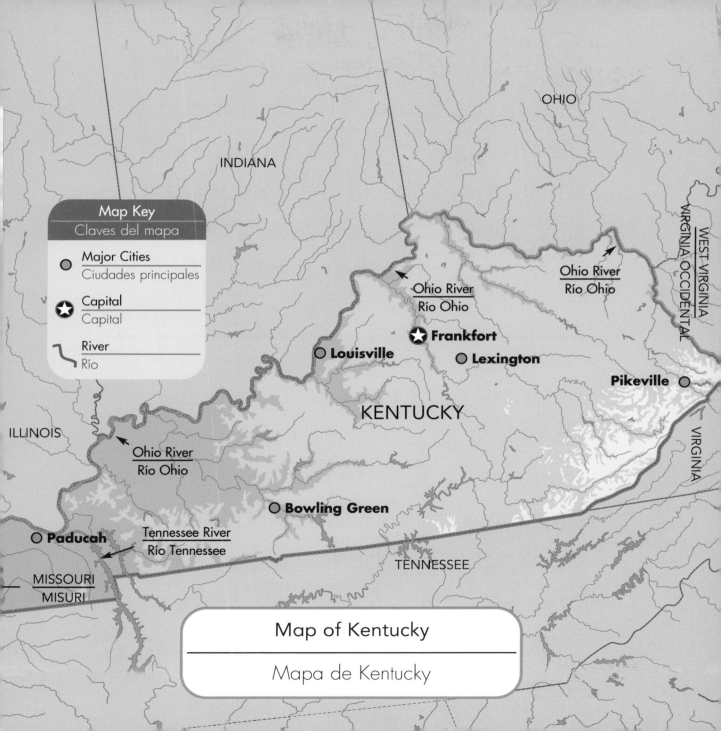

Kentucky is known as the Bluegrass State. The name comes from a type of grass that grows throughout the state. In spring, tiny, bluish purple flowers grow. They make the grass look blue.

Kentucky es conocido como el Estado *Bluegrass* (pasto azul). Este nombre viene de un tipo de hierba que crece en todo el estado. En primavera, la hierba se cubre de flores muy pequeñas de color violeta azulado. Estas florecitas hacen que la hierba parezca azul.

Kentucky's Bluegrass Area

Región de pasto azul de Kentucky

Kentucky is home to the longest cave system in the world. The Mammoth Caves are more than 340 miles (547 km) long. These caves were created by the water of rivers.

En Kentucky está el sistema de cavernas más largo del mundo. Las cavernas Mamut miden más de 340 millas (547 km) de largo. Estas cavernas fueron creadas por las aguas de los ríos.

Mammoth Cave National Park

Parque Nacional Caverna Mamut

Kentucky History

The name Kentucky comes from the Cherokee word *Ken-tah-ten*, or "land of tomorrow." The Cherokee have lived in Kentucky since the 1700s.

Historia de Kentucky

El nombre Kentucky viene de la palabra cherokee *ken-tah-ten* o "tierra del futuro". La nación Cherokee ha vivido en Kentucky desde los años 1700.

Cherokee Dancers in Kentucky

Danzantes cherokees en Kentucky

Daniel Boone was a pioneer. A pioneer is someone who explores a new land and settles there. In 1775, Boone crossed the Appalachian Mountains and guided many settlers into Kentucky.

Daniel Boone fue un pionero. Un pionero es alguien que explora y se establece en una nueva tierra. En 1775, Boone cruzó las montañas Apalaches y guió a muchos pobladores a Kentucky.

Daniel Boone

Abraham Lincoln was born on a Kentucky farm on February 12, 1809. Lincoln was America's sixteenth president. He led the country from 1861 to 1865.

Abraham Lincoln nació en una granja de Kentucky, el 12 de febrero de 1809. Lincoln fue el presidente dieciséis de los Estados Unidos. Lincoln lideró el país de 1861 a 1865.

Abraham Lincoln

Living in Kentucky

Bluegrass music began in Kentucky. Bluegrass is a type of music with Scottish, Irish, and African American roots. Many bluegrass events are held in Kentucky every year.

La vida en Kentucky

La música *bluegrass* comenzó en Kentucky. El *bluegrass* es un tipo de música que tiene raíces escocesas, irlandesas y afroamericanas. Cada año, se realizan en Kentucky muchos eventos de música *bluegrass*.

Bluegrass Musicians

Músicos de bluegrass

Kentucky has fun museums. In the Louisville Slugger Museum you can visit the factory that makes the bats for Major League Baseball. More than 2.5 million bats are produced here every year.

Kentucky tiene muchos museos divertidos. En el Museo Louisville Slugger puedes visitar la fábrica que hace los bates para las Ligas Mayores de Béisbol. Cada año, se producen allí más de 2.5 millones de bates.

GENUINE

J. A. "Bud" Hillerich

LOUISVILLE SLUGGER ®

A Giant Baseball Bat at the Louisville Slugger Museum

Un bate de béisbol gigante en el Museo Louisville Slugger

America's most famous horse race takes place in Kentucky. It is called the Kentucky Derby. The Kentucky Derby has been held every year since 1875.

La carrera de caballos más famosa de los Estados Unidos tiene lugar en Kentucky. Se llama el Derby de Kentucky. El Derby de Kentucky se ha realizado todos los años desde 1875.

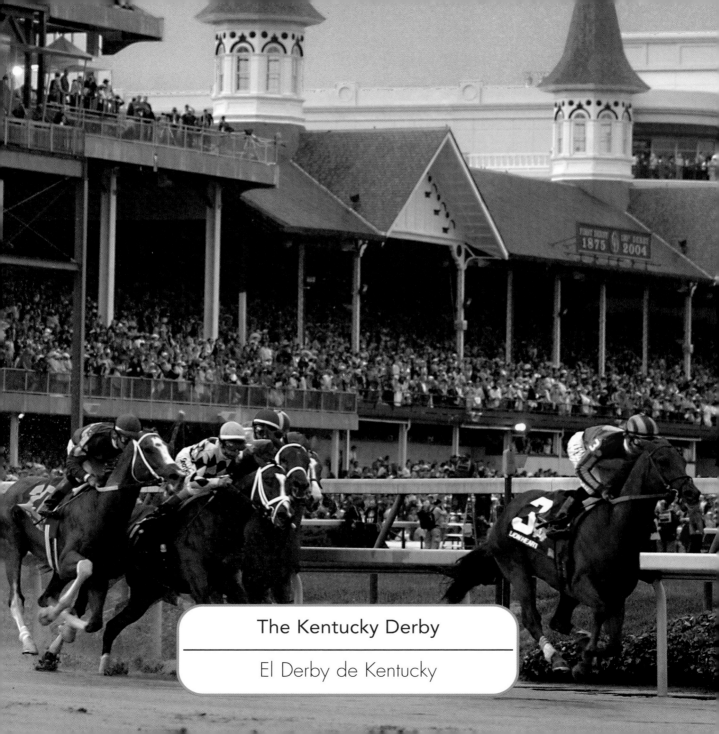

The Kentucky Derby

El Derby de Kentucky

Louisville, Lexington-Fayette, Owensboro, and Frankfort are important cities in Kentucky. Frankfort is the capital of the state.

Louisville, Lexington-Fayette, Owensboro y Frankfort son ciudades importantes de Kentucky. Frankfort es la capital del estado.

State Capitol Building in Frankfort

Capitolio del estado en Frankfort

Activity:
Let's Draw Kentucky's State Tree

The tulip poplar tree became Kentucky's state tree in 1994.

Actividad:

Dibujemos el árbol del estado de Kentucky

El tulipero es el árbol del estado de Kentucky desde 1994.

1

Draw two vertical lines, side by side. Draw the right line slightly longer.

Dibuja dos líneas verticales, una al lado de la otra. Dibuja la línea derecha un poco más larga.

2

Draw three curved lines. These lines give shape to the trunk and a branch.

Dibuja tres líneas curvas. Estas líneas les darán forma al tronco y a una rama

3

Show clumps of leaves by drawing two round shapes. Add four squiggly lines for other branches.

Para dibujar los grupos de hojas traza dos formas redondeadas. Agrega cuatro líneas quebradas en el lugar de las otras ramas.

4

Draw two more round shapes to outline the leaf clumps. Add more squiggly lines for more branches.

Dibuja otras dos formas redondeadas para mostrar otros grupos de hojas. Añade otras líneas quebradas para dibujar más ramas.

5

Draw five more round shapes to outline more clumps. Draw curved and bumpy lines all around the larger shapes.

Dibuja otras cinco formas redondeadas para mostrar más grupos de hojas. Traza pequeñas líneas curvas alrededor de las formas más grandes.

6

Erase extra lines. Add shading and draw smaller leaves.

Borra las líneas innecesarias. Sombrea y dibuja algunas hojas pequeñas.

Timeline | Cronología

Timeline		Cronología
Mississippian people disappear from the Kentucky region.	**1700**	Los nativos misisipianos desaparecen de la región de Kentucky.
Dr. Thomas Walker finds the Cumberland Gap.	**1750**	El Dr. Thomas Walker encuentra el paso Cumberland.
Kentucky becomes the fifteenth state of the Union.	**1792**	Kentucky se convierte en el estado quince de la Unión.
Kentucky legislature votes to remain in the Union.	**1891**	La legislatura de Kentucky vota la permanencia del estado en la Unión.
Bud Hillerich makes the first Louisville Slugger bat.	**1884**	Bud Hillerich fabrica el primer bate Louisville Slugger.
Martha Layne becomes the first woman to be elected governor in Kentucky.	**1983**	Martha Layne es la primera mujer en ser elegida gobernadora de Kentucky.
Kentucky starts a plan to clean up the environment.	**2000**	Kentucky comienza un plan de limpieza del medio ambiente.

Kentucky Events

April
Hoggs Falls Storytelling Festival

May
International Bar-B-Q Festival
in Owensboro
The Kentucky Derby in
Churchill Downs

June
The Great American Brass Band
Festival in Danville
Kentucky Shakespeare Festival
in Louisville

August
Kentucky State Fair in Louisville

September
Annual Gingerbread Festival
in Hindman
Bowling Green International Festival

December
Holiday Lights and Christmas
Village in Harlan

Eventos en Kentucky

Abril
Festival de narradores de cuentos de
Hoggs Falls

Mayo
Festival internacional de la barbacoa, en
Owensboro
Derby de Kentucky, en
Churchill Downs

June
Festival de las bandas de metales,
en Danville
Festival Shakespeare de Kentucky, en
Louisville

Agosto
Feria del estado de Kentucky, en Louisville

Septiembre
Festival anual de la galletita de jengibre,
en Hindman
Festival internacional de Bowling Green

Diciembre
Luces de los días de fiesta y Pueblo
navideño, en Harlan

29

Kentucky Facts/Datos sobre Kentucky

Population
4 million

Población
4 millones

Capital
Frankfort

Capital
Frankfort

State Motto
United We Stand,
Divided We Fall

Lema del estado
La unión hace la
fuerza

State Flower
Goldenrod

Flor del estado
Vara de oro

State Bird
Cardinal

Ave del estado
Cardenal

State Nickname
Bluegrass State

Mote del estado
Estado Bluegrass

State Tree
Tulip poplar

Árbol del estado
Tulipero

State Song
"My Old Kentucky
Home"

Canción del estado
"Mi viejo hogar en
Kentucky"

Famous Kentuckians/Kentuckianos famosos

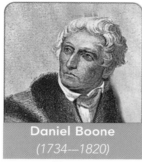

Daniel Boone
(1734—1820)

Pioneer
Pionero

Abraham Lincoln
(1809—1865)

U.S. President
Presidente de E.U.A.

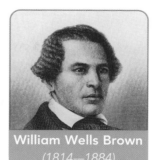

William Wells Brown
(1814—1884)

Abolitionist and writer
Abolicionista y escritor

Loretta Lynn
(1935—   )

Singer
Cantante

Muhammad Ali
(1942—   )

Boxer
Boxeador

Mary T. Meagher
(1964—   )

Olympic swimmer
Nadadora olímpica

Words to Know/Palabras que debes saber

border
frontera

cave
caverna

grass
hierba

pioneer
pionero

Here are more books to read about Kentucky:
Otros libros que puedes leer sobre Kentucky:

In English/En inglés:

Kentucky
America the Beautiful
Second Series
by Stein, R. Conrad
Children's Press , 1999

Kentucky
One Nation
by Kummer, Patricia K.
Capstone Press, 2002

Words in English: 302

Palabras en español: 361

Index

B
bluegrass music, 18
Boone, Daniel, 14
borders, 6

C
Cherokee, 12
Civil War, 16

F
flag, 4

K
Kentucky Derby, 22

L
Lincoln, Abraham, 16

M
Mammoth Caves, 10

S
seal, 4

Índice

B
bandera, 4
Boone, Daniel, 14

C
Cavernas Mamut, 10
Cherokee, 12

D
Derby de Kentucky, 22

E
escudo, 4

F
fronteras, 6

G
Guerra Civil, 16

L
Lincoln, Abraham, 16

M
música bluegrass, 18